STREET RHYMES AROUND THE WORLD

·E·DITED·BY· JANE YOLEN

ILLUSTRATED BY 17 INTERNATIONAL ARTISTS

Wordsong

FOR FRANCES KEENE, A TRUE INTERNATIONALIST

Copyright © 1992 by Jane Yolen

Illustrations copyright © 1992 by Boyds Mills Press, Inc.

Published by Wordsong

Boyds Mills Press, Inc.

A Highlights Company

910 Church Street

Honesdale, Pennsylvania 18431

Publisher Cataloging-in-Publication Data

Main entry under title.

Street rhymes around the world / edited by Jane Yolen ;

illustrated by 17 international artists.

[40] p. ; col. ill. ; cm.

Summary: An illustrated anthology of jump-rope and other counting street

rhymes from seventeen countries.

ISBN 1-878093-53-3

1. Jump-rope rhymes. 2. Count-out rhymes—Juvenile literature.

(1. Count-out rhymes.)   I. Yolen, Jane.   II. Title.

398.8 — dc20   1992

Library of Congress Catalog Card Number: 91-66058

First edition, 1992

Book designed by Joy Chu

Distributed by St. Martin's Press

Printed in the United States of America

Table of Contents

Introduction 5

· · ·

Introduction

· · ·

When I was a little girl living in New York City, I played bouncing ball rhymes like "One, Two, Three A-Nation" and jumped double-dutch—with two girls twirling two ropes for me to jump—to the rhythm of "Teddy Bear, Teddy Bear."

Girls and boys in New York and other American cities still use those same rhymes, nearly fifty years later, only now there are international double-dutch contests and new verses have been added.

When I started to collect the rhymes for this book, from books and from friends who had been brought up in different countries around the world, I was delighted to find that girls and boys everywhere play similar games. They bounce balls, jump rope, swing, count on their fingers and toes, choose up sides, and hide-and-seek using rhymes that may be particular to their own countries and their own customs but can be enjoyed by children everywhere.

Here are just a few of those rhymes set down especially for you, along with pictures drawn by artists from the countries where the rhymes originate.

Not all languages are written in Roman alphabet letters. Some languages, such as Danish, use written characters that are unique to their alphabets. Others, such as Greek, Hebrew, Russian, Chinese, and Japanese, have their own alphabets. For languages such as these, we have made a phonetic translation, or *transliteration,* of the words so you can "hear" how these rhymes sound.

—Jane Yolen

BRAZIL

1. Circle, little circle,

We'll all twirl around.

Let's do a half-turn,

A half-turn we'll do.

1. *Ciranda, cirandinha*

   Vamos todos cirandar.

   Vamos dar a meia volta,

   Volta e meia vamos dar.

2. *O anel que tu me deste*

   Era vidro e se quebrou;

   O amor que tu me tinhas

   Era pouco e se acabou.

3. *Senhora Dona _____,*

   Entre dentro desta roda,

   Diga um verso bem bonito,

   Diga adeus e vá-se embora.

2. The ring that you gave to me
   Was of glass and it broke;
   The love that you had for me
   Was small and it's over.

3. Mrs. _____,
   Come into the circle,
   Recite a pretty little verse,
   Say good-bye and go out. —circle game

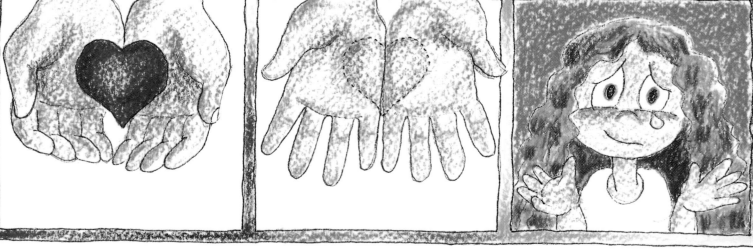

With thanks to Steve Yolen

INDIA (Tamil language)

Kai veesamma kai veesu,
Kadaikku pogalam kai veesu,
Mittai vangalam kai veesu,
Medhuvai thingalam kai veesu.

Wave your hand, wave your hand,
Let us go to the shop, wave your hand,
Let us buy some candy, wave your hand,
Let us eat it slowly, wave your hand.

—hand-waving game

8

Nila Nila Odi va,

Nillamal odi va,

Malai medhu Yeri va,

Malligai poo kondu va.

Moon, moon, come to me,

Come to me without delay,

Climb over the mountain and come,

Bring me jasmine flowers.

—*calling-the-moon game*

With thanks to Ranjani Krithivasan

ISRAEL

Bo elai parpar nechmad,
Shev etzlee al kaf hayad.
Shev tanuach al tirah . . .
Veta'oof bechazarah.

Come to me, nice butterfly,
Rest in the palm of my hand.
Sit, rest, don't be afraid . . .
And fly away again.

—*Hebrew finger game*

Alef
Beys
Giml
Dolid
Kokh mir in
a tepl fleysh.
Nisht keyn sakh,
Nisht keyn bisl,
Nor a fule shisl.

A
B
C
D
Cook for me
A pot of meat.
Not a lot,
Not a little,
But a whole bowl full.

—*A counting-out rhyme in the Yiddish language, which was once popular among Jewish children and adults in Eastern Europe, many of whom immigrated to Israel*

With thanks to Amir Cohen

JAPAN

Zui zui zukkorobashi

Goma, miso, zui, chatsubo ni

Owarete to-ppin-shan

Nuketara, don-do-ko-sho

Tawara no nezumi ga kome kutte

Chu, chu, chu, chu

Otto-san ga yonde mo

Okka-san ga yonde mo

Ikiiko na shi yo

Ido no mawari de ochawan kaita no dare?

12

Zui zui zukkorobashi

Goma, miso, zui, chatsubo ni

You're being chased by a big tea caddy . . .
    to-ppin-shan,

If you quit and go away, don-do-ko-sho

The mouse will eat the rice in the big straw bag,

Chu, chu, chu, chu,*

Even when Father calls it,

Even when Mother calls it,

It will not listen to them,

Who broke the rice bowl by the well?

—circle game

* sound of mouse squeaking

REPUBLIC OF RUSSIA

Na zlatom cryeltse sidelly
Tsar, tsarevich, karoll, karollevich,
Sapojnik, partnoy,
Kto tee budish takoy?

On a golden step sat
The Tsar, his son, king, prince,
Shoemaker, tailor.
Who are you going to be?

—counting-out rhyme for hide-and-seek

14

Raz, dva, tree, chiteery, pyat,

Vishel, zaychek, pagulat.

Vdrug ahotnic vebegiyat

Pramo v zaychika strillayat.

Peech pach oy oy oy!

Oomeraet zaychik moy.

Privizley evo v bolneetsu,

Paterial on rukovitzu.

Privizley evo domoy,

Okazalca on zhevoy.

1,2,3,4,5—

The rabbit went for a walk.

Suddenly a hunter ran out

And shot the rabbit.

Pow! Pow! Ouch, ouch! ouch!

My rabbit was dying.

The hunter took him to the hospital.

The rabbit lost his mitten.

The hunter brought him to his house.

And the rabbit got well.

—*counting-out rhyme for hide-and-seek*

With thanks to Iness Tsipman, Nelly Gofman and Barbara D. Goldin

PEOPLE'S REPUBLIC OF CHINA

Xiǎo Míng, xiǎo Míng,
Xiǎo xiǎo Míng Míng,
Shàng shàng
Xià xià
Zuǒ zuǒ
Yòu yòu
Qián qián
Hòu hòu
Yì liǎng gè
Pīng pāng qiú!

Little Ming, little Ming,
Little little Ming Ming,
Up up
Down down
Left left
Right right

Front front
Back back
One two each
Ping-Pong ball!

—*clapping game*

With thanks to Allison Chiu McGuirk

Xiǎo pí qiú, xiāng jiāo lí,
Mǎn dì kāi kuá èr shí yī,
Èr wǔ liù, èr wǔ qī,
Èr, bā, èr jiǔ, sān shí yī.

A little ball, a banana, a pear,

Twenty-one flowers looking everywhere,

Two five six, two five seven,

Two eight, two nine, thirty one.

—*counting rhyme or jump-rope rhyme*

With thanks to Louise Y. Wang

MEXICO

A la víbora, víbora
de la mar, de la mar,
por aquí pueden pasar.
Los de adelante corren mucho
y los de atrás se quedarán,
tras, tras, tras . . .

To the sea snake we will play,
we will play,
you can come and pass this way.
The ones in front run very fast,
and the ones behind will stay,
stay, stay, stay . . .

Una mexicana,
que fruta vendía,
ciruela, chabacano,
melón o sandía . . .

A Mexican woman,
selling fruit,
melon and plums,
and cantaloupe too . . .

18

Campanita de oro,
déjame pasar,
con todos mis hijos,
menos el de atrás,
tras, tras, tras . . .

Little golden bell,
please let me pass,
with all my little children
except the one who's last,
last, last, last . . .

¿Será melón?
¿Será sandía?
¡Será la vieja del otro día!
Día, día, día . . .

Will it be plum?
Will it be lemon?
Will it be cantaloupe or maybe melon?
Melon, melon, melon . . .

—play song

With thanks to Pedro Garcia Moreno

ENGLAND

Seesaw, sacaradown,
Which is the way to Londontown?
One foot up, the other foot down,
That is the way to Londontown.

—seesaw rhyme

"Fire! Fire!" said Obediah.

"Where? Where?" said Stephen Clare.

"Behind the rocks," said Doctor Fox.

"Put it out," said Jimmy Trewin.

"That's a lie," said Jacky Treffry.

—jump-rope rhyme

Eggs and ham,

Out you scram.

—counting-out rhyme

GREECE

Gyro gyrovoli
mesa sto pervoli,
heria, podia stin grammi,
olee kathountai stin gi.

Around the round path
in the orchard,
hands, feet on the line,
everybody sit on the ground.

—*play song*

Adé milo sti milia,
Ké heretam ti griya;
Posa hronia thé na ziso?
Ena, dio, tria, téséra.

Go, apple, to the apple tree,
And give my compliments to the old woman;
How many years shall I live?
One, two, three, four.

—*counting-out rhyme*

With thanks to Panos Chrysanthis and Areti Papanastasiou-Chrysanthis

GERMANY

Eins, zwei, Polizei;
Drei, vier, Offizier;
Fünf, sechs, alte Hex;
Sieben, acht, gute Nacht.
Neun, zehn, Capitän;
Elf, zwölf, einige Wölf.

One, two, police;
Three, four, officer;
Five, six, old witch;
Seven, eight, good night.
Nine, ten, captain;
Eleven, twelve, some wolves.

—counting rhyme

Dreimal eiserne Stangen,

Wer nicht läuft wird gefangen.

Dreimal eiserne Schnitz,

Wer nicht läuft wird gesitzt.

Dreimal über den Rhein,

Wer nicht läuft ist mein.

Three times iron bars,

He will be caught who doesn't run far.

Three times iron posts,

He who doesn't run gets caught most.

Three times over the Rhine,

He who doesn't run is mine.

—tag game

REPUBLIC OF ZAMBIA

Icipyolopyolo ca bana ba nkanga apo!

Tapali.

Apo!

Toleni!

The guinea-fowl chick says it is there!

It is not.

There!

Take it up!

—hide-and-seek game

Ntonkale pansi,

Pansi pa ima lole,

Lole icimbilumbilu,

Cuni cikulu ca isa,

Ca kumana Ngoŵi.

Ngoŵi twende ku mapili,

Ku mapili kwa Sitoka,

Umwine ta ngesa.

A lesa ne maunga,

Maunga e Toka.

E e e e o!

Let us dig down,

Up comes a shrew.

The shrew is like a horned caterpillar.

A big bird has come,

As big as Ngowi.

Ngowi, let us go to the hills,

To the hills where Toka's father lives.

He himself hasn't come.

He comes with the wilderness,

The wilderness is Toka.

E e e e o!

—*mealtime song*

DENMARK

Pandebeen,
Øiesteen,
Næsebeen,
Mundelip,
Hagetip,
Dikke, dikke, dik!

Brow-bone,
Eye-stone,
Nose-bone,
Mouth-lip,
Chin-tip,
Dikke, dikke, dik!

—face game

Skoe min Hest!

Hvem kan bedst?

Det kan vor Præst!

Nei mæn kan han ei!

For det kan vor Smed,

Som boer ved Leed.

Shoe my horse!

Who can best?

Why, our priest!

Not him, indeed!

But our smith can,

He lives at Leed.

—toe-counting rhyme

NATIVE AMERICA/Cheyenne

Huchdjeho niochdzi'!

Huchdjeho niochdzi'!

Mata-etanio-o

Ini-stoni-wahno-tziyo,

Ehenowe, h'm-h'm-h'm!

Come, ye woodrats, here to me!

Come, ye woodrats, here to me!

Now the timbermen draw near,

Hither stealing, creeping hither,

Now I hear them, h'm-h'm-h'm!

—*swinging song*

(The Cheyenne people used to make swings from strips of buffalo hide, which they would hang from tree boughs. Men, women, and children would swing in pairs, standing face to face on leather swings, feet braced against their partners'. There also would be a circle of onlookers sitting around them.)

FRANCE

Trois fois passera,
La dernière, la dernière;
Trois fois passera,
La dernière y restera.

Three times by she passes,
The last, the last;
Three times by she passes,
The last stays here.

—game with arms raised as a drawbridge

Celui-ci a vu un lièvre,

Celui-ci lui a couru après,

Celui-ci l'a attrapé

Celui-ci l'a mangé,

Celui-là n'a rien eu.

Il a dit à sa mère:

"Je n'en ai pas eu, je n'en ai pas eu!"

This one saw a hare,

This one ran after it,

This one caught it,

This one ate it,

This one got none of it.

And he said to his mother:

"I had none, I had none!"

—*finger-counting rhyme*

REPUBLIC OF ARMENIA

Elim, elim, ep elim,
Good oodim, gangar tranim;
Havgit hanim pone tunim;
Tarr jinjogh.

Who am I? I am me,
Sowing grass, when I eat seeds.
I lay eggs in my nest,
That's where I roost when I rest.

—*counting-out rhyme*

34

Meg, yergoo, yergunnas;

Yerec, chors, choranas;

Hinc, vets, vernas;

Yoten, ooten, ooranas;

Innin, dacenin, jam yertas;

Dacen yergoo, hats geran.

One, two, grow tall.

Three, four, round as a ball.

Five, six, reach up high.

Seven, eight, don't scratch the sky.

Nine, ten, time for mass.

Eleven, twelve, lunch at last.

—*counting rhyme*

With thanks to Diana Der-Hovanessian

THE NETHERLANDS

Hik sprik, sprouw,
Ik geef de hik aan jou;
Geef de hik aan een ander man,
Die de hik verdragen kan.
Iikh ben het.

Hiccup-ikkup sprew,
I give the hiccup to you.
Give the hiccup to another man
Who can stand it better than you can.
You are it.

—*counting-out rhyme*

36

Rood wit blauw,

De koning en zijn vrouw,

De koning en zijn dochtertje,

Koffiedik,

Af ben ik!

Red white blue,

The king and his wife,

The king and his little daughter,

Coffee grounds,

I am out!

—*counting-out rhyme*

With thanks to Marten Cornellisen

UNITED STATES

Teddy bear, teddy bear,
Turn around,
Teddy bear, teddy bear,
Touch the ground,
Teddy bear, teddy bear,
Touch your shoe,
Teddy bear, teddy bear,
Say how-di-do,
Teddy bear, teddy bear,
Go up the stairs,
Teddy bear, teddy bear,
Say your prayers,
Teddy bear, teddy bear,
Turn out the light,
Teddy bear, teddy bear,
Say good night.

—double-dutch jump-rope rhyme

Red, white, and blue,
Tap me on the shoe;
Red, white, and green,
Tap me on the bean;
Red, white, and black,
Tap me on the back;
All out!   —double-dutch jump-rope rhyme

One, two, three a-nation,
I received my confirmation
On the day of declaration,
One, two, three a-nation.
                    —bouncing ball rhyme

ABOUT THE AUTHOR

Jane Yolen is the author of more than one hundred books for children, young adults, and adults. Her *Owl Moon*, illustrated by John Schoenherr, won the 1988 Caldecott Medal. She is also the author of *An Invitation to the Butterfly Ball* and *All in the Woodland Early*, both available from Caroline House, an imprint of Boyds Mills Press. The mother of three grown children, Ms. Yolen lives with her husband in Hatfield, Massachusetts.

ABOUT THE ILLUSTRATORS

Brazil: CLAUDIUS S.P. CECCON is the executive secretary of CECIP (Popular Image Creation Centre) in Rio de Janeiro, a nonprofit organization that creates education materials for the Brazilian poor. Originally from Italy, he currently lives in Rio de Janeiro.

India: JAGDISH JOSHI, born in Goarkhpur and now a resident of New Delhi, is the art director of *Writer and Illustrator,* a quarterly journal of the Association of Writers and Illustrators, based in New Delhi.

Israel: ELISHEVA GAASH, a free-lance artist, was born in Czechoslovakia and immigrated to Israel when she was two years old. She resides in Jerusalem.

Japan: KAORU ONO, born in Tokyo and currently living there, is a professor at Tokyo University of Art & Design.

Republic of Russia: SERGEI TUNIN is the art director and deputy editor in chief of *Vesiolie Kartinki (Happy Pictures)*, a children's magazine based in Moscow. Born in Blagoveshensk, he now resides in Moscow.

People's Republic of China: JIANG CHENGAN is the deputy executive editor of art for Foreign Languages Press, Beijing. He was born in Xiuyan, Liaoning Province, and resides in Beijing.

Mexico: DIEGO ECHEAGARAY, designer and illustrator, is a native and current resident of Mexico City.

England: JILL BENNETT, a free-lance artist and writer, was born in South Africa and now resides in London.

Greece: VASSO PSARAKI, born in Athens, is a free-lance artist living in Holargos.

Germany: CHRISTOPH ESCHWEILER, a free-lance artist, is a native of Cologne and now resides in Aachen.

Republic of Zambia: VINCENT MAONDE is the resident artist of The Livingstone Museum. Originally from Lusaka, he now lives in Livingstone.

Denmark: SVEND OTTO S., born in Copenhagen, is a free-lance artist living in Leire.

Native America/Cheyenne: IVAN J. SMALL SR. is an artist and retired rancher from the Northern Cheyenne Tribe of Montana. He was born near Kirby, Montana, and lives in Lodge Grass.

France: ANNIE BONHOMME, a free-lance artist and a native of Rouen, resides in Bry Sur Marne.

Republic of Armenia: ROUBEN MANOUKIAN is a free-lance artist who was born in Yerevan and currently lives there.

The Netherlands: ANNEMARIE VAN HAERINGEN was born in Haarlem and is a resident of Amsterdam. She works as a free-lance artist.

USA: CHRIS L. DEMAREST, a native of East Hartford, Connecticut, is a free-lance artist residing in Southport, Connecticut.

Jacket and Title Page: JEANETTE WINTER, a free-lance artist, is from Chicago, Illinois, and currently lives in Frankfort, Maine.